Ugenia Lavender

The One and Only

Geri Halliwell
Illustrated by Rian Hughes

MACMILLAN CHILDREN'S BOOKS

This is a work of fiction. These stories, characters, places and events are all completely made-up, imaginary and absolutely not true.

Ugenia Lavender X

First published 2008 by Macmillan Children's Books

This edition published 2009 by Macmillan Children's Books
a division of Macmillan Publishers Limited
20 New Wharf Road, London N1 9RR
Basingstoke and Oxford
Associated companies throughout the world
www.panmacmillan.com

ISBN 978-0-330-45433-9

Illustrations by Rian Hughes
Brain Squeezers by Amanda Li

1 3 5 7 9 8 6 4 2

A CIP catalogue record for this book is available from the British Library.

Printed and bound in the UK by CPI Mackays, Chatham ME5 8TD

Contents

To Bluebell. Little girl, big imagination.

Dear Reader

I have loved reading since I was a little girl - books have always been my great escape!

When I write stories about Ugenia, I feel like I'm going on a fantastic adventure. I start with an idea . . . and I never know how it's going to end until I get there. It's like Ugenia Lavender has a life of her own and I get lost in Ugenia's world, where anything can happen!

Ugenia's friends and family are all people we'd recognize in our own lives, and I hope all readers, young and old, will have fun with Ugenia and all her friends.

Ugenia is both flawed and inspirational - she sometimes acts up, and isn't afraid to ask for what she wants, but when she fails at anything she tries again, and always with a big smile! Perhaps Ugenia Lavender is a bit like me - or maybe even you!

I hope you grow to love her as much as I do.

Geri xx

Geri Halliwell shot to fame with the Spice Girls, a global music phenomenon selling over 55 million CDs.

She has travelled extensively as a United Nations Goodwill Ambassador with particular interest in issues affecting women and children, and she has had two bestselling autobiographies published.

Geri lives in London and has a daughter, Bluebell Madonna.

Books by Geri Halliwell

Ugenia Lavender

Ugenia Lavender and the Terrible Tiger

Ugenia Lavender and the Burning Pants

Ugenia Lavender: Home Alone

Ugenia Lavender and the Temple of Gloom

Ugenia Lavender: The One and Only

1

Ugenia Lavender

Saves the Planet

It was a Monday morning, and the end of autumn. The leaves were just about to take their final bow and fall from the trees, lining Cromer Road with what would look like a layer of golden nutty cornflakes.

Ugenia was ready for her mum to start moaning about how the leaves were such a nuisance, blocking up the outside drains and littering the garden. Ugenia, however, found the golden leaves rather useful – especially for art projects at school. Somehow they always came in handy.

Actually, the leaves on the trees should have dropped weeks ago – winter was just around the corner – but in the last few weeks the weather had got strangely

warm. In fact it felt as hot as summer.

At breakfast Ugenia's father, Professor Lavender, who was a consultant at the Dinosaur Museum and a specialist in pretty much everything, discussed the weather issue over scrambled eggs. He said it was due to climate change – global warming. Ugenia had no idea what that meant.

Ugenia went to school thinking about what he had said. It probably wasn't that important, she thought. Besides, there was nothing she could do about the weather, was there? Except wear appropriate clothing, right?

Ugenia went to her classroom for the first lesson of the day, with Mr Columbus. He was a new teacher at Boxmore Hill Junior School, who assisted Ugenia's main teacher,

Mrs Flitt, when she had lots of work to do. He was always very serious and he stuttered, as he was nervous about impressing Mrs Flitt and the rest of the class. Ugenia thought he looked rather odd for a teacher, with his long messy hair in dreadlocks, and he smelt a bit like compost. He was also quite boring, particularly when he droned on about sheep farming in the Outer Hebrides in Scotland, or milking cows, or the quality of soil. All she would hear was blah blah blah.

Ugenia was sitting with her best friends – Bronte, Rudy and Crazy Trevor – in the back row, writing notes back and forth

to them. Just silly things like 'you smell like rotten cabbage and have a face like a gerbil' to Rudy – things that only best friends were allowed to say to each other, because they knew they were only joking. Rudy did, however, have a rather strange-shaped face, especially when he gathered food in the sides of his cheeks. He also had a very skinny, long body, which made his head look extra big. He owned a pet gerbil

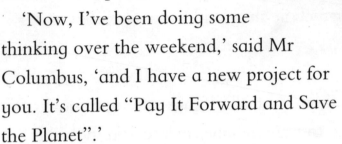

called Germaine, who he loved so much that sometimes he would sneak Germaine to school in his pocket.

'Now, I've been doing some thinking over the weekend,' said Mr Columbus, 'and I have a new project for you. It's called "Pay It Forward and Save the Planet".'

Suddenly Ugenia's ears pricked up. Ooh, save the planet – now this sounded interesting. It was like something Hunk Roberts did in the movie *Return of the Onion Savages*, she thought.

Hunk Roberts was Ugenia's favourite action hero, who was always saving people from things. Ugenia loved a school project

– it was like having a mission impossible, except you got marked on it.

'Shh!' Ugenia hissed at her friends. 'This sounds cool.'

Rudy, Bronte and Crazy Trevor stopped giggling and began to listen to Mr Columbus attentively.

'Let me explain,' continued Mr Columbus. 'I don't know if any of you ever watch the news or read the paper, but if you don't, I'm sure your parents will confirm that we live in very strange times. There is lots of pollution, crime, starvation, poverty and war in the world. These are all very grown-up subjects that cause an immense amount of unhappiness in the world we live in, and I am here to tell you that this is your world – it belongs to you! So you have a responsibility to make it better.'

There was a hush throughout the classroom. Everyone suddenly seemed to find Mr Columbus interesting for a change.

'What I want you to do is to make a difference to the world you live in,' Mr Columbus went on. 'Think of how you can Pay It Forward and Save the Planet. It's like having a savings account by investing in your futures today.

'On Friday I want you to show the class how and what you did to pay it forward. You can cover any topic – whether it's the environment, people's health, the homeless, or perhaps some research or ideas you have to make the world a better place. I want to get you out there interacting and thinking about the world you live in,' he said. 'Although this does sound a little overwhelming, remember it just takes the first tiny step to climb a mountain. So, kids, Pay It Forward and Save the Planet.'

'Wow, this sounds fabulous,' said Rudy.

'Great,' said Ugenia.

'Very nice,' said Bronte.

'Er . . . yeah,' mumbled Crazy Trevor.

☆

There were just four days till Friday morning, when they would be presenting their project, so, on Tuesday lunchtime, Ugenia, Rudy, Trevor and Bronte had decided to make a start and were discussing the Pay It Forward and Save the Planet project.

'I think I'm going to recycle all the

rubbish at my dad's shop,' said Rudy. (Rudy's parents ran a corner shop on Leavesden Road, which certainly created a lot of rubbish.) 'I'm going to insist my parents start separating their rubbish into special bins so that things like bottles and cardboard can be recycled.'

'I think I'm going to collect unwanted clothes and shoes from all my neighbours and send them to poor people in Africa,' said Bronte. 'Some Africans have to walk for miles in bare feet.'

'And I'm going to help slow down global warming,' said Crazy Trevor. 'Apparently we make so many gases with all the stuff we use it makes the world heat up like a greenhouse.'

'Wow, Trevor, that sounds really smart,'

said Bronte. 'What exactly are you going to do to help?'

'Well, erm, like I'm going to stop eating broccoli and baked beans for a start,' Crazy Trevor said proudly. 'So hopefully I'll stop letting off any gas myself and then if I catch anyone else letting one off I'm gonna give 'em what for and they will be fined. And I will give the money to my new foundation – the No More Toxic Gas Foundation! Like it?'

'Very nice,' said Bronte.

'Er, yeah,' said Rudy.

Meanwhile Ugenia said nothing – she was too busy thinking about what she could do to help pay it forward.

'What are you going to do, Ugenia?' asked Rudy.

'Erm, I'm still thinking about it,' said Ugenia, who so far hadn't come up with a single idea.

'Well, you'd better get a move on,' said Rudy, pulling Germaine the gerbil from his pocket. 'We only have a few days to do it.'

Germaine was very wriggly and loved to fidget. He had sandy-coloured fur with a black tip on the end of his long tail.

'Isn't he just the cutest thing?' said Rudy.

'Very nice,' said Bronte.

'Looks like a little rat, if you ask me,' laughed Trevor. 'My cat would love to eat him up for breakfast.'

'That's not funny, you oaf,' said Rudy, giving Germaine a kiss. 'Germaine is not a rat and is the most precious thing in the world to me.'

Suddenly, Germaine scrambled on to Rudy's hair. Anoushka, who was sitting on the lunch table opposite, began to scream.

'A rat, eeeeeeuh! Help me! Do something!' she shrieked, jumping on to the chair and waving her arms hysterically.

Sebastian, who was sitting next to her, lunged forward at Rudy's hair. Ugenia tried to block him, but it was too late.

Germaine panicked and sank his very sharp teeth into Ugenia's finger, leaped on to the floor and ran across the canteen. There was chaos as people began chasing the darting and panicking Germaine.

'Stop him!' screamed Rudy.

Ugenia cornered Germaine with her hands but it was too late. Germaine backed away and disappeared through a tiny hole in the wall.

'Noooooooooo!' cried Rudy. 'Germaine, come back! What am I going to do? He'll be eaten up or lost forever.'

'It's not the end of world. Maybe he'll make some new friends,' said Trevor.

'It is the end of the world for me!' cried Rudy with his head in his hands. 'He's my best friend. He only bit Ugenia cos he was scared.' Rudy began to sob.

'Don't worry, you've still got us as friends,' said Ugenia, trying to be helpful. 'And we'll find him, won't we, guys!'

'Yeah, er, don't worry about it,' said Trevor, who felt a bit uncomfortable seeing another boy cry, so he patted Rudy on the back.

☆

That afternoon Ugenia found herself rather distracted during lessons, as she kept scouring the floor on her hands and knees, looking for Germaine. Rudy's pet had been missing for an hour and so far he was nowhere to be seen.

Rudy had been looking so miserable since Germaine had vanished that Ugenia couldn't help but worry about her best friend. What can I do? she thought as she watched Rudy sink further into despair.

Ugenia's mind was a blank with any ways to make it better for Rudy, and she hadn't started on her Pay It Forward and Save the Planet project either. Everyone else seemed to have great ideas.

'I'm going to organize a sponsored walk around the playing field to help the homeless,' said Liberty.

'I'm going to get everyone to give up their pocket money for a whole month and give it to Cancer Research,' said Max.

'I'm going to put up posters that I drew myself and have had printed, to stop people chopping down trees in the rainforest,' said Sita proudly.

Ugenia felt slightly uncomfortable. All

their projects sounded fantastic. I need some inspiration, she thought. I wonder if Hunk Roberts ever got stuck. He made it look so easy. Maybe I should ask my dad? After all, he is a professor and he is very clever and he knows pretty much everything.

☆

After school Ugenia jumped on her red bike and sped down Boxmore Hill, past the twenty-four-hour, bargain-budget, bulk-buyers' supersized supermarket and into the town centre. She went straight to the Dinosaur Museum, where her dad worked. It was an old grey building with two stone gargoyles peering down from the roof.

Ugenia wandered through the large, stone building, under the huge diplodocus skeleton, past a stegosaurus horn, down the

stairs and along a dusty, dark corridor.

She tiptoed quietly past three men in white coats, wearing their do-not-disturb frowns as they peered down at a tiny piece of what looked like a dinosaur bottom. Ugenia knocked on her father's door, which said:

PROFESSOR
EDWARD LAVENDER
DINOSAUR CONSULTANT
AND
SPECIALIST IN PRETTY
MUCH EVERYTHING ELSE

'Enter!' called Professor Lavender.

'Dad, I need your help for my school project,' said Ugenia. 'It's called Pay It Forward and Save the Planet,' she explained, 'and quite frankly, Dad, I haven't got a clue where to start.'

Professor Lavender's eyebrows knitted together as he rubbed his chin and began to think intently. 'Hmm, let me see. How about doing it on the investigation of the migration of turtles in the Galapagos

Islands? Or the destruction of the ice cap and the rehousing of polar bears. Or the reconstruction of the River Nile? Or draining the sewage from the River Thames? Cleaning the birds involved in the latest oil-slick accident or the decommissioning of jumbo jets and their turbo engines? Stop whale hunting, excess fishing, bear dancing in Turkey, donkeys in circuses, children working when they shouldn't be? There's plenty to choose from, Ugenia,' said Professor Lavender.

Ugenia gulped. It all sounded so grown up and complicated and her mind went blank.

Suddenly Charlie Darwin, her father's main assistant, came in. 'Er, sorry to bother you, Professor Lavender. I just wanted to remind you to turn the lights off and unplug your computer tonight as you'll be the last to leave.'

'Thanks, Charlie, good point! We want to save electricity, that's for sure!' said Professor Lavender.

'Why do you want to do that, Dad?' asked Ugenia. 'Is the Dinosaur Museum trying to save money?'

'Well, actually, Ugenia, yes, it does need to save money, but there is a far more important and bigger reason than that. This planet is running out of power,' explained Professor Lavender. 'To put it simply, it's best to turn things off when you're not using them. It could help save the planet.'

Ugenia stared at the lights overhead, and the computers and machines that whirred and glowed as they hungrily sucked the electricity out of the wall. Then suddenly, like a thunderbolt of lightning, she had a brainwave. 'Inspirational!' she cried. 'Save electricity and save the planet! That's what I'll do for my Pay It Forward project! Thanks, Dad!'

'Glad I could be of help,' said Professor Lavender. 'Now, let me give you some top tips on how to save the—'

But it was too late, Ugenia was almost

halfway down the corridor and running out of the building, ready to save the planet.

☆

As Ugenia lay in bed that night, just about to fall asleep, she suddenly realized she wasn't entirely sure how she was going to save electricity or find Rudy's gerbil. But before she could worry about it any more, she had dozed off. It had been a very long day.

The next morning, Ugenia leaped out of bed, ready to save the world as she sped to the bathroom and gave herself an extra-special toothpaste-advert smile. But as she

turned on her electric toothbrush, she suddenly thought, Isn't this a waste of electricity? She switched the toothbrush off and began to brush manually, proudly thinking of how she was saving the planet.

Then Ugenia hurried down the stairs ready for breakfast with her great-grandmother, Granny Betty, who was 101 years old. Granny Betty looked after Ugenia most mornings when her parents had gone to work. She was pretty special as she was a mixture of fun and wisdom. Ugenia poked at her scrambled eggs.

'Not hungry?' asked Granny Betty. 'You need to fuel up good if you want to think straight.'

'You're right, Gran,' said Ugenia. 'I do have so much to think about, what with saving electricity and saving the planet and trying to find Rudy's gerbil, Germaine.'

'Oooh, you have got a lot on your plate dear, you'd better eat up!' said Granny Betty as she handed Ugenia a piece of burnt toast with thick peanut butter on it. 'I think you have a better chance of saving the planet than finding Germaine.

Apparently the longer that runaway pets are gone, the slimmer the chances of ever finding them.'

Ugenia felt pretty glum as she packed her lumimous yellow rucksack for school and thought about what Granny Betty had said. 'Rudy will be heartbroken,' she said to herself. 'I mustn't give up on looking for Germaine.'

☆

That afternoon, Ugenia didn't focus much on her Pay It Forward project as she was too distracted by the fact that Rudy looked even more miserable, sadly holding his head in his hands and staring out of the window. She just had to find Germaine.

After school, Ugenia was just about to head off home, when her friend Bronte asked if she would come to watch her at swimming practice. Bronte had to do a jump off the big diving board for part of her swimming exam and was really scared. She was a very good friend of Ugenia's and was very smart, but sometimes she could be very shy and lacked confidence when it came to doing something new under pressure in front of other people.

'Sure,' said Ugenia. 'I can only come for a bit though. I have so much work to do on my Pay It Forward and Save the Planet project.

'Thanks, Ugenia,' said Bronte, and they walked to the swimming pool together.

Ugenia stood at the side of the pool as Bronte came out of the changing rooms, and watched as she climbed up the high ladder.

Bronte froze when she reached the top of the diving board. Ten minutes later and she was still standing on the edge, staring down at the pool beneath her. The other people queuing below her started to look up impatiently as they waited for their turn.

As Ugenia stared at Bronte, she realized how alone she must feel, standing up there in front of everyone, doing something new. Hmm, that takes real courage to jump in, thought Ugenia. Suddenly, like a thunderbolt of lightning, Ugenia had a brainwave. Encouragement! 'Come on, Bronte, you can do it!' she shouted up at her.

But still Bronte didn't move. So Ugenia decided there was only one thing left to do . . .

Quickly she took off her skirt, boots and socks, pushed past the other people waiting and climbed up the ladder (only wearing her pants and a T-shirt, as she wasn't expecting to do any swimming that day).

Smiling, Ugenia took Bronte's hand. 'Come on, Bronte, let's do this together!' she cried as she looked down. She took a deep breath. 'One, two, three, jump!' shouted Ugenia. Then she and Bronte did the best gigantic leap off the diving board.

As they hit the water together, making the biggest, most humongous splash and drenching everyone watching, the crowd of other swimmers roared and clapped.

'Nice one!' smiled Ugenia as she pulled herself out of the pool and high-fived Bronte. 'Uh-oh,' she said as she saw Mrs Flitt, their teacher, who also taught PE, coming towards them.

'Where is your swimming costume?' said Mrs Flitt.

'Erm . . . well, it was that um –' stuttered Ugenia, not knowing what to say as her teeth chattered together.

'Go and get dry immediately before you

catch a cold,' said Mrs Flitt crossly.

'I was only trying to help,' muttered Ugenia under her breath as she walked to the changing room.

☆

That night, Ugenia got ready for bed in the dark as she was trying to save electricity. She tripped over in the process and put her pyjamas on inside out.

As she lay in bed, she suddenly realized that she hadn't really come up with any big amazing plan to save electricity for her Pay It Forward and Save the Planet project, and that she still hadn't found Rudy's gerbil, Germaine. But before she could worry about it any more, she fell asleep. It had been another very long day.

☆

On Thursday morning, Ugenia leaped out of bed. Things are much better once I've had a chance to sleep on them, she thought as she manually brushed her teeth and gave herself an electric-saving smile. I'm really gonna go for it today and get my project done.

In class, everyone was busy cutting out pictures, gluing, sticking, writing and adding the finishing touches to their projects, ready to present tomorrow.

Lara Slater, who had been Ugenia's number-one enemy when Ugenia started at Boxmore Hill School, came over to Ugenia's desk. They had sort of made up last term on Ugenia's birthday.

Ugenia had accidentally rubbed nettles on Lara's dad's head (thinking it was good luck) and she had wrongly accused Lara of stealing her lucky charm bracelet. Ugenia had apologized, and Lara had taken it all really well and hadn't been as horrible as she used to be. The fact that Lara wasn't giving Ugenia looks of disgust or contempt any more must mean they were sort of almost nearly friends, possibly.

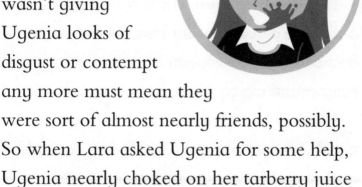

So when Lara asked Ugenia for some help, Ugenia nearly choked on her tarberry juice and spat it out all over her in shock . . .

'Ugenia, I need some guidance on what exactly qualifies as saving the planet,' said Lara stiffly.

'Well, I've only just started mine,' said Ugenia. 'But my dad told me that saving electricity was a very good example – you know, like turning the lights off when you've finished using them, because the world is running out of power,' explained Ugenia.

'That's very interesting,' said Lara.

'There's lots of other things too . . . like housing homeless Inuits or recycling glass bottles and paper . . .'

But before Ugenia could say another word, Lara had moved on to the next table and was chatting intently to Sebastian about his walk-to-work campaign, so Ugenia carried on working. However, she still couldn't quite get her Pay It Forward and Save the Planet project off the ground as she just felt so distracted by Rudy's long face – he looked more depressed than ever. Before she knew it, it was the end of the lesson and they were packing away their things.

'I look forward to seeing your presentations tomorrow!' said Mr Columbus.

Well, at least I've still got this evening to work on saving the planet, thought Ugenia. But first I need to sort Rudy out!

Ugenia had decided that since Germaine had decided to go AWOL (Absent WithOut Leave) the best thing to do was to provide Rudy with a new best friend – someone as good as Germaine if not even better. So when Ugenia got home, she emptied her money jar of all the loose change she had

collected over the last six months and it came to six pounds and sixty-nine pence. Then she knocked on Crazy Trevor's door and they jumped on their bikes to go and find Germaine's replacement. They sped down Boxmore Hill, past the twenty-four-hour, bargain-budget, bulk-buyers' supersized supermarket, all the way to the Bargain Bucket One Stop Pet Shop. It was right at the edge of town by the empty wasteland that had a small overspill of the reservoir running through it. The sign said:

AFFORDABLE FURRY FRIENDS
FOR THE WHOLE FAMILY

Ugenia and Trevor walked through the shop door and stared at the twenty budgies squashed into a tiny cage. There were almost a hundred fish stuffed in a tiny tank – there wasn't room for any of them to even swim without bumping into each other.

'This doesn't look very nice' said Ugenia.

'Yeah, it smells of wee,' said Trevor, holding his nose. 'But it is cheap.'

'Can I help you?' said a rather grumpy-looking man behind the counter, who had greasy hair, bad skin and was wearing a tight vest over a very round beer belly that was protruding over his trousers.

'Do you have any gerbils, please?' asked Ugenia in her best grown-up voice.

'Yeah, how many do you want?' grunted the man.

'Just one,' said Ugenia, who was taking even more of a dislike to this man.

'I'll give you a deal – three for a fiver. Is it to feed your snakes?' wheezed the man.

'No, it certainly isn't,' snapped Ugenia.

'It's to become the new Germaine for our very best friend, Rudy.' She felt even more disgusted by this man.

'Oh, right,' the man grunted. He opened the door to a very dirty cage and roughly grabbed a very frightened gerbil and popped it into a cardboard box. 'That will be three quid.'

Ugenia hesitated, then handed him the money. She picked up the box with Germaine number two in it and marched out of the shop, followed by Trevor.

'Trevor, we have to do something!' cried Ugenia. 'Those poor animals trapped in there in those tiny cages with that horrible stinky man!'

'Yeah, right!' said Crazy Trevor. 'Like what?'

Ugenia peered back through the window at the goldfish bumping into each other, the budgies with no room and the mice and gerbils ready to be fed to snakes. The grumpy man was now in a chair behind the counter, snoozing. What would Hunk Roberts do, she wondered.

'Ingenious! *The Great Escape*!' cried Ugenia. 'Set them free, of course! Trevor, they would be better out in the world, rather than in there being either suffocated or eaten for lunch!'

So Ugenia and Crazy Trevor crept back into the pet shop.

Crazy Trevor, who was very strong for a boy of his age, lifted up the budgie cage. Ugenia then loaded the mice and gerbil cage on top of it and Crazy Trevor staggered out of the shop, across the road and on to the wasteland. The grumpy man snoozed peacefully, oblivious to anything.

'He won't even miss them! I know his type,' cried Ugenia. 'He doesn't even like animals,' she finished as she opened the budgie-cage door. 'Fly free! Fly free!'

But the birds just sat there and didn't move.

'It looks like they're a bit scared,' said Ugenia. 'Encouragement, that's what they need. They need a bit of support, like Bronte jumping off the diving board!' Ugenia reached in and began taking each budgie out and throwing it up into the air.

Sure enough, each budgie flew up . . . before flying back towards the pet shop and slamming into the window. Then, a little dazed, they perched themselves on the pet shop's drainpipe.

'Oh, this is not working, Trevor. Let's try the mice and gerbils!' said Ugenia as she opened their cage. 'Run free, run free!' she shouted.

This time, the mice and gerbils

scampered eagerly into the wasteland.

'Fantastic, Trevor! They're free!' shouted Ugenia.

'Er . . . yeah,' said Trevor. Then they suddenly noticed a rather scraggy looking cat ready to pounce from a tree.

'Shoo!' snapped Ugenia, flapping her arms.

'Ah, let him eat one, Ugenia,' said Crazy Trevor. 'He does look a bit hungry, dunnee?'

'That's it. I've done with trying to help things that can't be helped!' said Ugenia as she snatched up the bag with Germaine number two in it. 'Besides, I have my Pay It Forward and Save the Planet project to do. I'm going home.'

And with that, Ugenia and Crazy Trevor

cycled back up Boxmore Hill. Ugenia said goodbye to Trevor and when she finally got home and plonked herself on the comfy couch, she gave the biggest sigh of relief, giving Germaine number two a squeeze.

'What a day!' said Ugenia. 'Now all I need to do is have my Pay It Forward and Save the Planet project done before supper!'

Suddenly the bell rang.

Granny Betty answered the door. It was Rudy. He came into the living room, looking more miserable than ever. 'I found Germaine at the end of class,' he said sadly.

'That's great!' cried Ugenia.

'Not really,' said Rudy. 'He was dead, stuck in a drainpipe,' he sobbed, hugging a parcel of newspaper to his chest (Germaine was wrapped inside it).

Ugenia stared at Rudy. She so wanted to make him feel better, but didn't know quite what to say.

'I know Germaine was very special to you, so perhaps you should give him a proper funeral, Rudy,' said Granny Betty, bringing in a tray of cookies and a large, empty matchbox. 'Ugenia, call your friends and let's give Germaine the send-off he deserves.'

With her 101 years behind her, Granny Betty had a lot of experience in making things better, and of funerals as well.

Ugenia quickly called Trevor and Bronte.

Fifteen minutes later Rudy, Ugenia, Crazy Trevor, Bronte and Granny Betty were in the back garden. Ugenia dug a tiny hole in the ground and lowered the large matchbox, which now was Germaine's new home, into the ground.

Rudy quietly whimpered as Crazy Trevor covered the matchbox over with soil.

'Would anyone like to say a few words?' asked Granny Betty.

'I've actually written a short poem,' said Bronte, unwrapping a

piece of paper that she took out of her pocket and beginning to read . . .

'Germaine, thank you for being such a
good friend;
I'm sorry your life has come to an end.
You were so brave and kind and free,
Such a great pet for our friend, Ru-dy.
We're so sad you had to die.
We'll miss you lots, big kiss goodbye . . .'

Everyone clapped, then suddenly there was a gust of wind. It was as if the trees were listening and were just waiting for their cue. The golden leaves began to fall, covering Germaine's grave in what looked like golden nutty cornflakes, and leaving the trees bare, like skinny skeletons.

Ugenia snapped a small branch from the silver birch tree and stuck it in the ground. 'In memory of Germaine, the greatest pet ever!' she said, giving Rudy a big hug.

'Thanks, Ugenia, I feel much better,' said Rudy.

'That's good,' said Ugenia. 'Because I actually have someone who needs a new owner. His name is Germaine number two.'

And Ugenia pulled out the new gerbil from her luminous yellow rucksack.

'Wow, thanks so much, Ugenia – he looks very cute,' said Rudy, giving Germaine the second a big hug.

'And I've even managed to get some black paint from my dad's garage to paint his tail,' said Crazy Trevor, trying to be helpful. 'So he'll look just like Germaine the first.'

'Thanks, Trevor, that was very thoughtful,' said Rudy.

The sun was beginning to set and it was starting to get a bit cold, so everyone said their final goodbyes to Germaine and went back inside. The winter weather had finally decided to come. Rudy, Bronte and Trevor then said goodbye to Ugenia.

'Big day tomorrow!' said Bronte.

'Yeah, can't wait to show you my project,' said Rudy.

'The project!' cried Ugenia as she shut the door behind them and gasped.

Ugenia sat on the hall stairs and stared blankly at the walls. I haven't even started my Pay It Forward project, she thought.

Granny Betty came into the hall and brought Ugenia a cup of hot tarberry juice.

'Are you OK, Ugenia?' she asked.

'Ooh, Gran, I've really messed up. I haven't even started my Pay It Forward and Save the Planet project. I've been so caught up with trying to find Germaine. And after all that he's dead now anyway.' Ugenia put her head in her hands. 'Granny Betty, why did Germaine have to die?' she asked sadly as big fat tears rolled down her face.

'Everything dies eventually, Ugenia,' said Granny Betty. 'Like the leaves on the trees – everything has its season. It's the circle of life. The leaves fall, making space for the new ones that come in the spring. A bit like Germaine – he had his time, and then made way for a new gerbil to come along.'

'Ooh, well, I hope I stay around longer than the leaves do,' said Ugenia.

'Of course you will, look at me, I'm a hundred and one!' smiled Granny Betty. 'That's why it's so important to take care of ourselves and the planet we live on, and cherish each moment, realizing what's important and what's not.'

'Wow, that was pretty deep, Gran, thanks,' said Ugenia.

Ugenia then had some spaghetti bolognaise for supper with her parents. Just before bed, she walked round the house and thought about what her gran had said about taking care of ourselves and the planet. She then unplugged all the gadgets that were still left on, even though they weren't being used.

Yes, I can start looking after the planet right now by saving some electricity, smiled

Ugenia to herself. She then said goodnight to her parents, who were playing cards in the dining room, and went off peacefully to bed . . . it had been a very long day.

☆

The next morning Ugenia was woken up by the sound of voices shrieking in the house.

'Oh my goodness, I'm late for work! Why didn't my alarm go off? It's unplugged!' cried her mother, who worked on Breakfast TV as a presenter.

'Oh, noooooooo. My research . . . it's all gone . . . my computer has turned itself off – it's been unplugged. How did this happen?' shouted her dad.

Ugenia then went down to the kitchen to find the floor flooded.

'The fridge-freezer is unplugged!

Everything has melted!' screamed her mother as she slipped in a puddle. 'All the food has gone off.'

'Er, that was me. I unplugged everything,' said Ugenia. 'I was trying to save electricity – the planet is running out of power.'

'Well, I can see you were trying to be helpful,' said Pandora Lavender. 'But perhaps you should have asked us first.' Then she suddenly burst out laughing. 'Go and get ready for school. We'll talk about this later. I have to get to work.'

In no time at all, Ugenia got to school. It was presentation time . . .

'I'm very excited to hear all about what

you've done for your Pay It Forward and Save the Planet projects' said Mr Columbus. 'So let's start with Sebastian . . .'

Sebastian pulled out a big display on the benefits of not chewing gum and how they don't do it in Singapore.

Then Rudy brought in his recycling containers and described how recycling had been working in his dad's shop.

Sita showed the posters she'd made to stop trees being chopped down in the rainforest and said how she'd been planting new trees with her parents.

Mr Columbus went through everyone's project till there were only two people left – Lara Slater and Ugenia Lavender.

'Well, I've come up with a very original idea,' said Lara. 'It's to save electricity. I've been turning lights off around the house when people aren't using them. Saving the planet's energy is saving the planet.' Lara looked proud as she showed the class pictures of drawings of lightbulbs, fridges and TVs.

'Injustice! That was my project idea!' cried Ugenia 'I told her that's what I was going to do!'

'OK, Ugenia,' said Mr Columbus. 'You seem to be very passionate about it, so let's have a look at what you've done. Come up and show us. Perhaps you ladies could compare notes with each other. It's very common for a good idea to be thought of by more than one person, you know.'

'Er, well, I'm not quite ready,' said Ugenia.

'Not ready?' Mr Columbus spluttered.

'But you've had all week, Ugenia. Why aren't you ready?'

'Well, I've had a lot going on . . . erm, erm,' stammered Ugenia.

'She was busy being my swimming coach!' interrupted Bronte quickly. 'Thanks to Ugenia's encouragement I can now jump off the big diving board, which previously I was too scared to do.'

'And she saved some animals,' said Crazy Trevor. 'She helped these poor little creatures who were living in smelly cages to find a new home on the wasteland!'

'And she helped me get over the loss of a very dear friend with a fabulous funeral, and found me a new friend too,' announced Rudy.

'Well, it does sound as if you have been

very busy, Ugenia,' said Mr Columbus. 'What with personal coaching, releasing animals into their natural environments and helping others. I did say I wanted you all to get out there interacting and thinking about the world you live in, and it looks like Ugenia Lavender has been a living example of just that.' Mr Columbus smiled. 'Ugenia hasn't just talked about it, she has gone out and actually done it! It's the little things that can make a big difference – remember I said it takes just the first tiny step to climb a mountain? Well done, Ugenia. I'm very impressed with your project – you really have taken steps to give something to the world. Being kind and supporting others is really what paying it forward and saving the planet is all about.'

'Thank you, Mr Columbus,' beamed Ugenia.

At the end of class Mr Columbus was thanking everyone for their efforts, when suddenly Crazy Trevor put his hand up . . .

'I forgot to tell you,' he started. 'I've come up with a brilliant idea on how to save the planet. I started doing it this morning.'

'Fantastic Trevor,' said Mr Columbus. 'Please share it with us.'

'Recycling yesterday's toilet paper! What d'ya think?'

The class went quiet.

'Like it!' said Rudy.

'Love it,' said Ugenia.

'Very nice,' said Bronte.

uGenia Lavender

Big News!

Hello

Wow that was a sad week, wasn't it? Poor Rudy. Germaine is now in gerbil heaven. Actually, do gerbils go to heaven? Is there even a *special* gerbil heaven. I'll ask my dad. I imagine heaven for gerbils would be a place where they wouldn't get stuck in drainpipes or eaten by snakes!

Actually, there was some good stuff too that happened. Bronte passed her swimming exam – cool. Rudy got a new pet and Trevor, well . . . I have to tell you his recycling yesterday's toilet paper hasn't quite caught on. (Bless him for trying to save the planet – every little thing helps, right?!)

And my mum and dad forgave me for flooding the kitchen. Saving electricity is a good thing, but I suppose it's best to ask your mum and dad first before you unplug anything!

There are many ways to help save the planet we live on. I learned so much this week about it. Mr Columbus is right – we kids have a responsibility to care for our future.

Anyway, for those of you who haven't heard the news – my mum's pregnant, and her belly is getting bigger every day. I don't know when this supposed baby is going to come out. I think she's made the 'expecting a baby thing' up. She's just been eating way too many of Granny Betty's cakes, if you ask me.

Anyway, I'm off to plant some

trees with Sita on the green – cool, eh!

Big XO

Ugenia Lavender XX

Ugenia Lavender

Ingenious Top Tip

If we all kept our own doorsteps clean, the whole world would be tidy

Sometimes the whole world can look a mess – a bit like my bedroom. But if you focus on something small, the big task ahead doesn't seem so scary. If everyone did something small but kind for their friends, it would make the world a better place.

2

Ugenia Lavender

Wanted Dead or Alive

It was Thursday, on a cold and crisp November evening. Ugenia was extremely excited, as, even though there was school tomorrow, she had been allowed to stay up late because tonight there was going to be a lunar eclipse, which only ever happened occasionally. (This is when the moon passes through the earth's shadow.)

Ugenia sat on her windowsill in her Hunk Roberts action-hero pyjamas and

stared intently at the night sky. It was all very still, almost as though the sky was holding its breath and the stars were on their best behaviour.

Sure enough, the moon looked as though it was submerging into a black glove as it disappeared into the shadow of the indigo sky.

Wow, that's amazing, thought Ugenia. There's a whole galaxy out there!

Ugenia suddenly felt quite small as she continued to gaze in wonder at the universe that loomed above her. Then, just as Ugenia was about to climb down from the window, she saw a green flash of light that began to zigzag across the sky. It whizzed and whirled until it stopped abruptly then began to freefall at high speed towards the ground. Faster and faster it plunged, nearer and nearer, getting bigger as it approached, heading straight for Ugenia's back garden . . .

There was a loud whoosh and the large green light disappeared behind the garden shed.

'Wow! What on earth was that?' gasped Ugenia, who was now almost frozen in disbelief. 'Did I see that? Or am I dreaming?' Ugenia pinched herself, which hurt, so clearly she wasn't dreaming.

Ugenia decided there was only one

thing to do and that was to investigate. So quickly she sneaked downstairs with her father's torch and wandered into the back garden.

Ugenia felt a little scared but tried to pretend she wasn't. As she walked forward she could see the strange light glowing at

the back of the garden shed. Ugenia tiptoed down the path quietly, trying not to make any sound as she approached the silver birch tree and peered behind the shed.

Ugenia froze. There in front of her was a steel capsule that looked like a dustbin, wedged right on top of the compost heap. The dustbin thing glowed and made a very strange whirring sound like a broken washing machine. It had the large initials ET on it. Then all of a sudden there was a mighty hiss and a metal lid flipped up and smoke oozed out.

'Er, hello?' stammered Ugenia, not even sure to who or what she was saying hello.

There was no reply except that the machine gave one last metallic groan . . .

Ugenia began to tiptoe backwards. Perhaps I should get my dad. This looks a bit weird, she thought, when suddenly she heard a whimpering from the dustbin capsule thing. 'Go away! Go away! Go away! I want to be alone!'

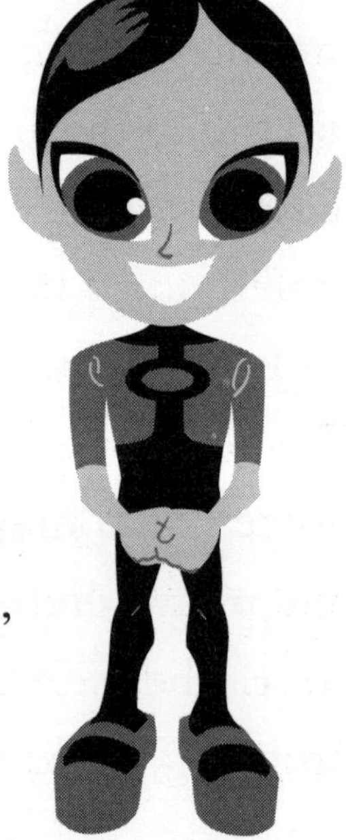

Did I just hear something? thought Ugenia.

'Yes, yes, yes, you did,' replied the voice.

'Who said that?' said Ugenia, thinking, How did it know what I was thinking, whatever it is?

'I'm Edie . . . Edie . . .

Edie . . . Edie Titchmarsh, that's who! See my initials, ET, on my vessel,' said the voice that seemed to be hiding.

Ugenia thought about this for two seconds, maybe three. 'Ah, that explains everything. For a minute I thought you were a space alien,' sighed Ugenia with relief. 'AS IF! Silly me – that green light must have been part of the eclipse. I think your dustbin must have been zapped by it. There's no need to hide any more, it's over!'

The voice in the dustbin was silent.

'Just come out, Edie,' called Ugenia. 'There's nothing to worry about. Just come inside my house, we can have a cup of tea and phone your parents. Then they can come and pick you up. I'm sure they're probably really worried about you,' she continued. She was beginning to feel a little impatient.

Ugenia turned her back on the dustbin, as if to go, crossing her arms and tapping her feet impatiently. When she looked back, there in front of her was a very strange-looking little girl with large green eyes and scaly purple skin. She was only half as tall as Ugenia, with a huge smile on her face. 'You mean I can phone home?' the little girl beamed.

'Er, yeah, sure,' said Ugenia, trying not to be rude and stare too much. That eclipse must have turned the little girl's skin a funny colour. And she's very small for her age, thought Ugenia. 'Look, maybe we'd better put this dustbin away,' said Ugenia, dragging it into the shed.

Edie laughed. 'That's not called a dustbin,' she said. 'It's my spacepod! I was on an expedition from the Planet Varton, but I ran out of petrol.'

'Yeah, yeah, OK, whatever floats your boat,' said Ugenia, thinking Edie must still be in shock from being frazzled by the eclipse, she was coming out with such gibberish. 'Just come inside,' coaxed Ugenia. 'You can phone home to get your mum to come and get you.'

So Ugenia and Edie wandered into the house. It was very quiet and still.

'Everyone must have gone to bed!' exclaimed Ugenia. 'My mum's got an early start. She works on Breakfast TV. You've probably seen her – Pandora Lavender – she's very popular.'

'TV?' questioned Edie, but Ugenia didn't hear her as she went into the kitchen and put the kettle on.

'You just make yourself at home,' Ugenia called, placing some cookies on a plate. 'And I'll make us a nice cup of tea, then you can call your mum.'

Three and a half minutes later, Ugenia brought the tray of tea and goodies into the living room, only to find Edie lying stiff as a board, up on the bookshelf, fast asleep.

Hmm, strange place to sleep, she must be

exhausted, poor little thing, thought Ugenia as she lifted her down and covered Edie with a blanket on the sofa. It can't hurt to stay overnight. We can call her mum in the morning. She stared at Edie, who was still rigid, except she was snoring like a diesel-lorry engine.

Ugenia wandered upstairs to bed, thinking what a strange night it had been and feeling pretty exhausted herself . . .

☆

The next morning, Ugenia bounced out of bed feeling full of beans. She stared in the mirror, giving herself her special toothpaste-advert smile. Casually she got dressed and hummed as she went downstairs for breakfast. Ugenia burnt a piece of toast, so she threw it in the dustbin.

'The dustbin! Edie!' gasped Ugenia, suddenly remembering the house guest who had been frazzled by the eclipse.

'Morning, Ugenia,' said her dad, looking up from his newspaper.

'Morning, Dad, have you seen my friend Edie?' said Ugenia.

'Can't say I have,' said Professor Lavender as he flicked on Channel 24. 'Your mum's on telly.'

Ugenia looked across just as her mother's face appeared on screen.

'Breaking news just in,' said Pandora Lavender from a cream couch. 'An unidentified flying object was spotted shooting through the sky last night. It's reported that the pilot is a very dangerous alien. If you are approached by this aggressive being, please run, and call the police immediately. This is a Code Red warning as this alien has landed without permission and has intentions to cause terror, damage and destruction. Therefore this alien is WANTED, DEAD OR ALIVE.'

'That sounds serious,' said Dad.

'What does?' said Ugenia, who hadn't really been paying much attention as she was too busy looking for Edie under the sofa.

'Never mind, Ugenia,' said Professor Lavender. 'Just be careful. There can be some real weirdos out there.'

'Tell me about it,' said Ugenia, who was beginning to think Edie was slightly rude, since she must have left without saying goodbye.

'I'm off to work, Ugenia. Now don't be late for school,' said Professor Lavender.

'OK, Dad, I'll be leaving in a minute,' said Ugenia, following him into the hall and closing the front door behind him. Ugenia was all alone in the house. Suddenly she heard a rustling sound. It sounded as though it was coming from

down the hallway. Ugenia peered back into the kitchen, only to find Edie glugging a whole family pack of tarberry juice. She was covered in food wrappers and the entire contents of the fridge were half-eaten and all over the floor.

'Edie! What are you doing?' cried Ugenia. 'You can't just raid someone else's fridge and, besides, I've been looking for you.'

'Ooh, I was just a bit peckish like, and um you know,' said Edie, proudly giving a large belch and rubbing her round tummy. 'Nice one!' She smiled.

'I think we'd better call your mum to come and get you.' Ugenia frowned.

'I've already tried,' said Edie. 'But I couldn't get a connection. Perhaps I could try again a bit later. If I could just relax here for a bit that would be grand.'

'Er, well, em,' muttered Ugenia, who was beginning to think this house guest was a bit rude and overstaying her welcome. 'OK, but promise not to make a mess,' said Ugenia. 'I've got to go to school.'

'Me come too! Me come too! Me come too!' cried Edie.

'Sorry, but you're too young,' said Ugenia. 'Besides, you can't come dressed like that. That green catsuit is just too much for school. I'll be back later, just behave yourself.'

☆

Ugenia went through the school day in her usual manner, with Rudy, Bronte and Trevor. There was a huge buzz going around the whole school. All everyone could talk about was the dangerous alien that was terrorizing the town centre.

'He'll vaporize you,' said Rudy.

'He'll swallow you whole,' said Trevor.

'Sounds dangerous,' said Bronte.

'Sounds fascinating,' said Rudy.

'Sounds fantastic,' said Trevor.

'Sounds like rubbish if you ask me,' said Ugenia. 'AS IF!'

Ugenia was sick of this constant buzz about a stupid alien that didn't even exist. Besides, she had poor little Edie Titchmarsh to think about. Ugenia was busy trying to come up with an ingenious brainwave, when suddenly a little figure, swamped in Ugenia's best purple fleece hoody and wearing dark shades, approached them . . .

'Who's that?' asked Rudy.

'Who's what?' asked Ugenia, looking up.

'I'm Edie . . . Edie . . . Edie . . . Edie Titchmarsh,' smiled Edie. 'I'm Ugenia's house guest. I'm the foreign-exchange student.'

Rudy looked at Ugenia. 'Foreign-exchange student?'

'Don't ask,' Ugenia raised her eyebrows. 'She's a little fragile right now. But yeah, she has been staying with me.'

'Looks a bit weird to me,' sniggered Trevor as Edie's odd eyes poked out over the big black shades.

Unfortunately Edie was attracting attention from everyone . . .

'Ooh, look at that weirdo,' said Sebastian.

'Shorty,' giggled Sita.

'Funny face,' whispered Liberty.

'Freaky,' laughed Chantelle and Anoushka.

'Different!' said Max.

'That's enough!' shouted Ugenia. 'Shut up! You're not all that normal-looking yourselves,' she cried, suddenly feeling she'd better protect Edie. Besides, it wasn't her fault she looked like that. It was the stupid eclipse. And Ugenia knew exactly how rotten it felt to be different – like when she had first arrived at Boxmore Hill School from her travels in Egypt and Lara Slater had been picking on her.

'We gotta go, we have a phone call to make,' said Ugenia, dragging Edie away and walking her back to 13 Cromer Road as fast as she could.

☆

As soon as Ugenia got home, she went into the kitchen to make a sandwich. It looked like a bomb had hit the place. The fridge was now completely empty and the cupboard was bare. 'Edie?' cried Ugenia. 'Edie? What have you done?'

But Edie seemed to have disappeared and suddenly Ugenia's mum was walking through the door. 'Ugenia Lavender!' screamed Pandora. 'What on earth have you been doing? Look at this mess?'

Ugenia just stood there blankly. 'I don't understand how it happened,' she said remorsefully. 'It wasn't me. It must have been Edie. I told her not to make a mess.'

'Well, you'd better be more responsible with your friends in future and clean this up this instant,' said Pandora Lavender furiously. 'I'll pop over to Uncle Harry's. Let's hope he has some spare food since you've eaten all ours!'

'All right, Mum, but it's not fair,' huffed Ugenia. She stomped upstairs to her bedroom, slammed the door and sat down on her bed before folding her arms crossly.

Just at that moment, Ugenia heard a whimpering sound from beneath her. Ugenia peered under the bed to see Edie, curled up in a ball shivering. 'What's wrong, Edie?'

'I don't feel very well,' Edie cried.

'I'll call your mum, you need to go home,' said Ugenia.

'I've been trying all day, but the line was engaged,' said Edie, who was becoming more distressed.

'Do you know what's wrong with you?' asked Ugenia.

'I just feel very weak,' said Edie. 'I have this uncontrollable appetite, yet no matter how much I eat I don't feel full and nothing seems to give me any energy.'

Ugenia looked thoughtful. Maybe I

should ask my dad, she said to herself. After all, he is a professor and he is very clever and he knows pretty much everything. 'Edie, just relax, I'll be back as soon as I can.'

So Ugenia rushed down the stairs and jumped on her red bike. Quickly she sped down Boxmore Hill, past the twenty-four-hour, bargain-budget, bulk-buyers' supersized supermarket and into the town centre. She went straight to the Dinosaur Museum, where her dad worked. It was an old grey building with two stone gargoyles peering down from the roof.

Ugenia wandered through the large, stone building, under the huge diplodocus skeleton, past a stegosaurus horn, down the stairs and along a dusty, dark corridor.

She tiptoed quietly past three men in white coats, wearing their do-not-disturb frowns as they peered down intently at a tiny piece of what looked like a dinosaur

eyeball. Ugenia knocked on her father's door, which said:

PROFESSOR
EDWARD LAVENDER
DINOSAUR CONSULTANT
AND
SPECIALIST IN PRETTY
MUCH EVERYTHING ELSE

'Enter!' called Professor Lavender.

'Hi, Dad,' said Ugenia, bursting in. 'I really need your help.'

'Is this about that brontosaurus nostril?' asked her father, giving Ugenia a kind smile.

'No,' said Ugenia. 'I think my friend Edie is ill.'

'What are her symptoms?' enquired Professor Lavender.

'Well, she is very weak,' said Ugenia.

'She has this uncontrollable appetite, yet no matter how much she eats she doesn't feel full, and nothing seems to give her any energy. Oh, and her skin is a really funny colour. I think she was zapped by the lunar eclipse last night.'

Professor Lavender looked intently at his daughter for a few seconds, and his eyebrows nudged each other. Then suddenly his face brightened up. 'Ah, this is like a Varton Reptoid. They suffer from extreme withdrawal if they are away from their planet, Varton, for more than a day, and they die, but of course that wouldn't apply to your friend, who's probably just got a weird tummy virus, unless she too is an alien from outer space!' chuckled Professor Lavender.

Suddenly at that second, like a thunderbolt of lightning, Ugenia had a brainwave.

'Incredible!' she said out loud. 'Edie really is from the Planet Varton!'

'Great,' Professor Lavender beamed. 'Now would you like to see that brontosaurus nostril?'

But Ugenia didn't hear him. She was already halfway down the corridor.

☆

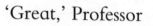

Ugenia cycled as fast as she could back up Boxmore Hill to 13 Cromer Road and to Edie, who was still lying under her bed, looking worse than ever. Ugenia then rang her friend Rudy and told him everything

– from the green light in the sky to how Edie was a Varton Reptoid and would die in less than twenty-four hours unless she got home to Planet Varton, but that her space capsule had run out of petrol!

'Rudy, I have a plan,' said Ugenia. 'It's a bit of a tricky mission impossible called "Edie Titchmarsh goes home". I need the best people for the job, dedication and loyalty, so call Trevor and Bronte for help, please,' said Ugenia in her best action-hero Hunk Roberts voice. 'Come over right away, if you can.'

☆

Ten minutes later, Rudy, Trevor and Bronte were in Ugenia's bedroom, peering under the bed.

'Are you sure she's friendly,' asked

Bronte, who felt a little uneasy with Edie's strange, scary big green eyes.

Edie began to sob uncontrollably, so Bronte quickly handed Edie her best hanky, which had a letter B embroidered on it.

'Thank you,' said Edie, giving Bronte back her hanky, which now had sticky orange stuff on it.

'Fabulous catsuit!' said Rudy.

'Er, yeah, bit weird skin though,' said Trevor, offering Edie a bite of his supersized caramel-fudge hard-candy lolly.

Edie gave a whimper and gulped the whole lot down.

'Ouch, she bit me,' cried Trevor.

'Oh, she's just hungry,' Ugenia told him. 'That's why we have to get her home, otherwise she'll be dead in a few hours.' Ugenia was just thinking hard about what they should do to help Edie, when her mother called up the stairs.

'Supper, Ugenia, it's on the table!'

Ugenia turned to her friends. 'Take Edie downstairs and meet me in the garden shed,' she said. 'See if you can restart her spacepod dustbin-thing. And whatever you do, don't let my mum see you. She's cross enough with me as it is without me bringing home an alien, even if she is friendly.'

Ugenia went downstairs to find her mother watching the six o'clock Prime Fast evening news on Channel 24.

'More news in on the very dangerous alien,' said the reporter from behind a desk. 'The alien, as first thought, has been causing terror, destruction and despair, and is now damaging large fields by making strange circles that are flattening crops. We also have an eye witness, Farmer Hislop. Let's cut to him now . . .'

'Yes, it was awful,' a big burly man was saying. 'It was terrorizing everything in its path, so I pointed my gun at it and screamed, but it squirted this horrible orange sticky stuff all over me . . . it really hurt. Thankfully I jumped straight into my bath and I got it off. It was ready to kill me, I'm sure.'

'And news just in,' said the newsreader. 'We have further terror developments – there has been an alien abduction. Larry Smith, a tarberry-juice truck driver, has gone missing as well as all the contents of his lorry. This alien is wanted dead or alive. I repeat DEAD OR ALIVE. So the police have now given this as a Code Black.'

'Oh goodness, that sounds really serious,' said Pandora.

'Mum, I'm really not hungry,' mumbled Ugenia, who was too busy thinking of more serious matters – like how to get Edie home. It wasn't exactly as if her alien, Edie, was dangerous, was she? (Besides, she'd been with her pretty much the whole time, hadn't she?)

And with that, Ugenia legged it up the

garden to the shed, where Rudy, Bronte, Trevor and Edie were hovering around the metal dustbin.

'Well, it definitely has run out of petrol,' said Bronte, peering down a silver petrol tank.

'We could get some from the petrol garage up the road, right?' said Ugenia.

'Er, no, this doesn't seem to take ordinary petrol, it smells like something else . . . it's quite familiar, but I can't quite put my finger on what it is,' explained Bronte.

'Well, by my calculation we have only about one hour left to make this machine work,' said Rudy. 'Otherwise Edie the alien will have stayed more than a day, and she will be dead.'

'We have to do something!' said Bronte.

'Leave this to me,' said Ugenia, not knowing quite how she was going to sort this out.

Ugenia began to try and think as hard as she could, but nothing was coming to mind. She screwed up her nose and knitted her eyebrows together as if they were fighting. But to Ugenia's surprise, there was no thunderbolt of lightning, no brainwave, no flash of inspiration, nothing! This isn't like me, I normally think of something! she thought.

'Er, guys, I have to be honest here,' said Ugenia. 'I'm a little out of ideas on how to get special petrol for alien spacecrafts.'

Rudy then poured everyone a glass of tarberry juice from a flask while everyone tried to think.

'What about paint stripper?' said Bronte, pointing at an old can in the shed.

'Weedkiller?' said Rudy.

'Disinfectant?' said Bronte.

'Bleach?' said Rudy.

'Oven cleaner?' said Bronte.

'Detergent?' said Rudy.

'Washing powder?' said Bronte.

'Olive oil?' said Rudy.

'Beer?' said Trevor.

'OK, there's only one thing we can do and that's try all this stuff,' said Ugenia. 'We only have forty-five minutes left before Edie our alien is dead.'

Twenty minutes later, Rudy, Trevor, Ugenia and Bronte had gathered as many things as they could to try to use as petrol to make the spacepod dustbin-thing work.

Twenty minutes after that, the petrol tank had been filled with everything they could find, by which time the petrol tank was foaming and frothing but still not a squeak – nothing.

By this time, Edie Titchmarsh was howling and sobbing uncontrollably but nothing could console her. 'I want to go home! Edie go home! Edie go home!'

Ugenia, Bronte, Rudy and Trevor stared in disbelief. What could they do? There was only a matter of minutes left and they had failed to save her. All they could do was give Edie a huge hug as their little alien friend was about to die.

Rudy poured everyone a final glass of tarberry juice.

'I think it's time we called an adult,' said Ugenia.

'No, don't do that,' said Edie, snatching Trevor's tarberry juice and pouring it straight into the petrol tank.

And with that, the generator started whirling and hissing, and the spacepod dustbin-thing glowed with the familiar green light.

'That's what I could smell – tarberry juice!' exclaimed Bronte.

'Why didn't you use that in the first place, Edie?' asked Ugenia, who was a bit miffed that she'd gone to all that trouble. 'Oh, I needed a bit of a holiday,' smiled

Edie. 'And I wanted to stay a bit longer as I loved how nice you were to me, it was such a change. Normally everyone treats me like I'm weird, so we don't get on and I lose my temper. You can come and stay at mine next time.' Edie gave Ugenia a big hug. 'After all, you are my foreign-exchange student.' And with that she hopped in her spacecraft and in a flash was gone . . .

'No way!' said Rudy.

'Very nice,' said Bronte.

'Er . . . yeah, she was all right,' said Trevor.

'Well, I'm exhausted,' said Ugenia. 'It's me that needs a holiday!'

Ugenia was so tired, she thanked everyone for their support and went inside. Her mum and dad were sitting at the table watching the evening Prime Fast News on Channel 24.

'Well, it looks like the alien threatening terror and destruction was all a hoax!' said the newsreader sitting behind the desk. 'The supposed alien that was threatening our security was made up by a bunch of pranksters – the eyewitness, Farmer Hislop, was a bit of a loony and the missing lorry driver has been found, although he is under arrest as the tarberry juice hasn't. So we can all relax as the police have given us a Code Yellow,' smiled the newsreader.

'Thank goodness for that,' said Professor Lavender.

'Yes, thank goodness for that,' said Pandora.

'It's funny, after all this alien talk, I did a little research on that alien I mentioned earlier – the Varton Reptoid . . .' said Professor Lavender. 'Apparently they can do things as quick as a flash without you even knowing they're gone. And, even more scary, if they don't like you, when they get upset they can spray you with a horrid orange sticky stuff that can kill!' exclaimed Professor Lavender. 'It's a good job we've never met one, so we have nothing to worry about.'

'Nothing to worry about, Dad. Imagine one of us meeting a Varton Reptoid alien, AS IF!' smiled Ugenia.

Ugenia Lavender

Big News!

Newsflash . . . newsflash . . .
UGENIA LAVENDER MEETS ALIEN – AS IF!

Hi, guys

Do you think anyone would believe me if I did really? Come on, as if? They would probably rather believe I was mad and lock me up in a loony bin. Actually it might be quite fun to meet one . . .

So anyway, things got back to normal once Edie left, although I do keep finding food wrappers and orange snot in bizarre places – like down the back of the sofa and in the DVD player.

Oh, and my mum is so big, honestly. I've noticed people are extra nice to her once they realize she is pregnant. It's like suddenly she's extra special – anyone would think she's got the baby Jesus in her belly, but there's no room in my inn, no matter who this baby is. I'm not sharing. It can sleep in the shed. I don't feel that important any more – I feel pretty invisible when I stand next to her, quite frankly. I'm still secretly hoping it's a big lie and she has just been eating loads of pies and cakes when no one's around.

Fingers crossed. I'll keep you posted. Brrrr, it's so chilly, winter has finally come. The wind keeps biting my nose.

Big XO

Ugenia Lavender XX

Ugenia Lavender

Ingenious Top Tip

Even aliens can make nice neighbours

Wherever you live, we are all neighbours – you never know when you might want to borrow a cup of sugar. So it's always important to be neighbourly. People are terrified of things they don't understand – a bit like with Edie – but she was very nice once you got to know her!

3

Ugenia Lavender

The One and Only

It was morning of the first of December, and the ground was really crisp and hard with frost. The air was fresh and tense, as if it was holding its breath ready for snow to fall.

Ugenia Lavender woke up with her

biggest action-hero leap ever! Why such a monumental leap? Well, Ugenia Lavender was probably the most excited she had ever been in the entire nine years of her life.

She had only one day left until she would be taking her first trip ever to Hollywood in America. She had never been to Hollywood or America before. The exciting possibilities for amazing adventures seemed endless.

Ugenia looked in the mirror and gave herself the biggest American toothpaste-advert smile ever.

So, just why was she going to America? Well, Ugenia's mother was being sent on an assignment to interview a very famous actor called Bradley Litt and she was allowed to take her family with her. Ugenia's teacher, Mrs Flitt, had said it was OK to go, even though it was school time, because it was such a special trip (plus Ugenia had promised her an autographed picture of Bradley Litt).

Bradley Litt was very handsome and popular with Mrs Flitt. He was pretty popular with most ladies, including Ugenia's mother, who was very excited about meeting him. But Ugenia wasn't bothered about Bradley Litt – there were far more important people to meet. Hollywood was the place where they made a lot of movies and where film stars lived – especially her favorite action-hero movie star, the spectacular Hunk Roberts. Ugenia loved Hunk Roberts and had seen every one of his films more than once.

Ugenia sighed to herself as she brushed

her hair. She loved Hunk Roberts, not just because he was handsome but because he was also very brave. In times of trouble and disaster he could always think of ingenious ways to overcome any problem. Hunk Roberts was Ugenia Lavender's inspiration!

Ugenia walked back into her bedroom and quickly got dressed. She knew that she would have a pretty good chance of meeting Hunk Roberts, because in the summer, when she was accidentally on a film set, she met a very famous film director, Steven Speilbug, who lived in

Hollywood and said he could introduce her to Hunk. Ugenia was practically bouncing like an electric-powered rabbit. For the last month she had been talking non-stop to all her classmates about the trip, and today was the last day before she left, so she would be doing some extra-special gloating – especially in front of her enemy, Lara Slater, the big show-off. Lara was gonna be soooo jealous!

☆

After breakfast, Ugenia wrapped up warmly, gave her dog, Misfit, and her Granny Betty a kiss (her parents had already gone to work), and set off for school, ready for her big show-off day.

Ugenia entered her classroom and beamed. 'Finally I'm going! Tomorrow I will be off to Hollywood to meet Hunk Roberts! I'm almost there!' she called out to her friends Bronte, Rudy and Trevor. 'He's only one day away. Can you believe it?'

'Fabulous,' said Rudy.

'Very nice,' said Bronte.

'Er . . . yeah,' said Crazy Trevor.

It wasn't long before Ugenia's excitement spread like wildfire, and the rest of the class cooed in awe of Ugenia's very amazing trip.

'You're gonna have a great time!' said Sita.

'I wish I was going!' said Max.

'You're gonna meet loads of famous stars!' said Anoushka.

'Who's a very lucky girl' said Lara Slater with a half-pleased smile and cheeks that were flushed with envy.

'Thank you, everyone!' beamed Ugenia. 'I shall send you a postcard! And tell you about the extraordinary time I have when I meet Hunk Roberts!' She glowed with excitement. It was going to be amazing.

He is going to be so coolastically electric, dynamically fantastical, she thought. I know it – when I meet him I'm going to be blown away!

☆

The rest of Ugenia's day was filled with lots of compliments, excited interest and questions. Ugenia shone like a true show-off with all of the attention she was receiving. She could hardly wait for school to end and the next day to begin so she could travel to America. Ugenia said goodbye and that she would see everyone in a week's time. Then she went straight back home to Cromer Road, ready to help pack her case for Hollywood. As she walked through the door, Granny Betty gave her a bigger hug than usual.

'Wow, Gran, I can tell you're really going to miss me, aren't you?' said Ugenia, hugging Granny Betty back.

Granny Betty didn't reply except for, 'Go into the lounge. I'm going to make you a nice hot cup of tarberry juice.'

Ugenia walked through the door to find her mother and father sitting on the sofa with very long faces. Ugenia's mother had her feet up and was rubbing her very swollen, very large, very pregnant belly.

'Ugenia, we have something to tell you,' said her father. 'As you know, your mother is expecting a baby and we were thinking he or she would come in a couple of months, but the doctor has said it looks like your little brother or sister is going to come early. So I have some bad news . . .

I'm afraid that we won't be able to go to Hollywood after all.'

'INJUSTICE!' cried Ugenia. 'That's so unfair. I was supposed to meet Hunk Roberts!'

'I'm so sorry, Ugenia,' Pandora Lavender said gently. 'I know you were looking forward to it, we all were.'

'That baby is just so selfish. It's ruined everything! I HATE THAT BABY! AND YOU! I HATE MY LIFE!' screamed Ugenia as she stormed upstairs and slammed the bedroom door, which made the whole house shake. Ugenia flung herself on the bed, thumped the pillow with rage and began to sob furiously. 'No Hollywood, no Hunk Roberts, I'm never gonna meet him, this is all that stupid, selfish baby's fault.' She then stared at her puffy red eyes in the mirror and began to feel very sorry for herself.

It's just so unfair, Ugenia thought. I knew this baby was going to be a pain, but this is ridiculous – it's spoiling things even before it's arrived. Imagine what it's going to be like when it's born. My life is ruined!

And with that, Ugenia put on her Hunk Roberts pyjamas, hid under her duvet and refused to go downstairs for supper. To make matters worse, Ugenia would have to go back to school tomorrow and face everyone with no Hollywood story to tell . . .

☆

The next day, Ugenia sloped out of bed and slowly wandered to the bathroom. She didn't give herself an extra-special toothpaste-advert smile when she looked in the mirror. Instead, she pulled a very big frown which said: 'I'm not going to meet Hunk Roberts . . . I hate my life.' Ugenia pulled on her big boots (they felt heavier than normal) and practically slumped down the stairs into the kitchen, feeling extremely glum.

'Morning, Ugenia,' said Granny Betty. 'I know you feel a bit disappointed about the trip, but things always happen for a reason, don't they? It's for the best, you know. I mean, we want to make sure that this little brother or sister of yours is nice and safe until he or she comes out, don't we? Now, be a big girl. You can make your own breakfast, can't you, love?' And with that, Granny Betty walked up the stairs with a large tray of eggs, bacon and pancakes. 'We really need to take great care of your mum,' Granny Betty called back over her shoulder. 'She needs lots of rest until that little baby is born.'

'INJUSTICE!' huffed Ugenia. 'What about me?'

I knew this was gonna happen, thought

Ugenia as she buttered a burnt piece of toast. It's all about that stupid, selfish baby. And I know it's only gonna get worse . . .

☆

As Ugenia dragged her feet into school, she knew that she was about to face a room full of smug smiles from some of her classmates, especially Lara Slater, who was going to love the fact that she wasn't going to Hollywood after all. Thankfully she met up with her best friends, Rudy, Bronte and Crazy Trevor, first.

'What are you doing here?' said Rudy.

'The trip's been cancelled,' Ugenia huffed. 'And all because that stupid baby has decided to come out some time this month instead of next month. It's made my mum unwell,' moaned Ugenia. 'This baby is so selfish, it has ruined my life already.'

'Oh dear, that's such a shame,' said Bronte.

'I know, now I won't be able to meet Hunk Roberts,' said Ugenia.

'Well, at least you can come carol singing with us and we can earn some cash!' said Crazy Trevor.

'And we can go shopping together,' said Rudy, trying to make things better. 'There're plenty of fun things to do here as well. Besides, it's Christmas in just a few weeks and we can make some excellent Christmas decorations!'

'Er, I suppose you're right,' said Ugenia, who really wasn't convinced at all. None of it sounded as good as meeting Hunk Roberts, but she decided just to go along with things. Meanwhile, there were other more immediate issues to deal with . . . like Lara Slater's huge, full-sized smug grin that was coming straight towards her . . .

'Oh dear, poor little Ugenia. I've just heard the news. I'm so sorry to hear your travel plans are cancelled. I suppose you won't get to meet your precious Hunk Roberts,' said Lara in her best pretend-I-care voice, but she clearly couldn't hide the delight that beamed through her eyes. 'I guess it's Boxmore for you, just like the rest of us. Never mind, I'm sure there'll be plenty of fun,' said Lara, who then gave Ugenia a false, reassuring squeeze on her shoulder before marching off towards Liberty and Anoushka, who were giggling triumphantly.

Ugenia's shoulders dropped in defeat.

The whole day carried on pretty much the same – with a mixture of sympathy and gloating from her classmates. Ugenia was glad when the school day was over.

As Ugenia got home, she found her mother lying on the sofa under soft lighting, watching a very dramatic film and resting a mug of tea on her big stomach.

Ugenia stared at her mother, who looked really tired and nothing like the glamorous woman who sparkled on television. She cringed as she thought of the selfish, greedy

baby growing inside Pandora's swollen belly, who was draining all her mother's energy.

'Hello, Ugenia, could you fetch me some biscuits? This baby is very hungry!' sighed her mother.

Ugenia said nothing. She went into the kitchen and brought her mother some ginger biscuits.

'Ooh, not those ones, the baby prefers chocolate chip,' giggled her mum as she gave her tummy a rub.

'Injustice! I'm not that baby's slave!' whispered Ugenia under her breath as she rolled her eyes. Ugenia got the chocolate-chip cookies, presented them to her mother and stomped upstairs in a huff.

☆

That evening, Ugenia decided to watch a bit of a Hunk Roberts movie – that always cheered her up.

'I'm sorry, Ugenia,' said her father, stopping her as she was about to put the DVD on. 'Your mother and I are just about to watch a birthing documentary.'

'Injustice!' shrieked Ugenia. 'That selfish baby is taking over everything – even the television!'

'Now, Ugenia, that's quite enough,' said Professor Lavender. 'You might like to watch it with us. It's very interesting, you know – it's all about how the baby comes out of the mother's womb, down the birth canal, and then, of course, the umbilical cord is cut and there's the what-to-do-with-the-placenta discussion.'

'La la la, not listening,' Ugenia said with her hands over her ears. That sounds disgusting! she thought. Revolting!

Ugenia left them to it and wandered into the kitchen, where she helped herself to some cold leftover spaghetti as her mother was too tired to cook that night. Ugenia sucked down the cold stringy pasta. Things couldn't get any worse, right?

☆

But unfortunately things did exactly that . . .

Ugenia found even more injustices and revolting baby-related annoyances leading up to Christmas than she could ever have imagined. Everything revolved around how her mother was and what the unborn thing was doing. Even Misfit seemed to spend all his time curled up next to her mother's swollen belly as if it was a heater.

It's all that stupid, selfish baby's fault, thought Ugenia as she wondered how she could get this baby to stop ruining her life. Normally Ugenia could think of an ingenious idea, but since there had been so many thoughts of injustices about the baby in her head there seemed to be no room for any inspirational ideas at all . . .

Then one Friday after school, just two weeks before Christmas, Ugenia decided to take her mind off the new, irritating arrival and go carol singing with Rudy, Bronte and Crazy Trevor up Cromer Road. They were all sitting in her upstairs den, discussing the Christmas carols they were going to sing.

'How about "We Wish You a Merry Christmas"?' said Rudy.

'Nah, too obvious,' said Ugenia.

'"Deck the Hall with Boughs of Holly"?' said Bronte.

'No, too jolly,' said Ugenia.

'"Little Donkey"?' suggested Rudy.

'Too naff.'

'"Mary's Boy Child"?' said Rudy.

'No way,' snapped Ugenia. 'I don't want to even think about babies, let alone *sing* about them, thank you very much.' Ugenia suddenly felt even more irritated. 'I can't concentrate,' she sighed. 'I can't get into this Christmas cheer knowing that I have that selfish baby about to demolish my life.' So Ugenia decided to take a break from this creative session to go to the loo – sometimes by stepping out of the room, the change really cleared her head.

As she sat down on the toilet seat she suddenly saw there was no paper. 'Injustice!' she cried. 'Doesn't anyone in this house know the importance of loo paper?

Well, I know exactly how that loo paper feels – neglected and unimportant! I wish my parents realized the importance of loo paper. Everyone is so preoccupied with that baby that this family is falling apart!'

Ugenia stared at herself in the mirror, realizing how important she used to feel when she was the only child. Except now she wasn't. And that was an impossible situation she couldn't change.

Then suddenly, like a thunderbolt of lightning, Ugenia had a brainwave.

'INGENIOUS!' she cried. 'I *am* the only child. It's a mission impossible!' And with that, she ran back into the den.

'Rudy . . . Rudy, it's time we had a mission impossible!' cried Ugenia. 'Somehow I have to remind my parents about the importance of being the only child. I need dedication and loyalty, and you're all the best people for the most difficult job yet.'

'Great to be of help,' Rudy said excitedly. 'I'll make a vision board!'

'Now that's a great idea!' said Ugenia, suddenly cheering up. Mission impossibles were always very useful and somehow made Ugenia feel like things had a chance to get better, even when things were falling apart – a bit like in a Hunk Roberts movie.

Rudy stood in front of a big sheet of paper.

'You need to think of ways to remind your mother that this baby isn't everything and that she still has a wonderful daughter,' suggested Bronte thoughtfully.

'Good idea,' said Rudy. 'And maybe if she realizes how important you are in their lives she won't think this baby is so significant.'

'Er . . . yeah, yeah, you're better than that boring baby,' said Crazy Trevor.

Rudy scratched his head and smiled, and wrote in big words . . .

THE IMPORTANCE OF BEING UGENIA, THE ONE AND ONLY CHILD

1. MAKE THEM NEED YOU - DO HOUSEWORK AND STUFF ROUND THE HOUSE SO THEY DEPEND ON YOU AND CAN'T LIVE WITHOUT YOU.

2. MAKE THEM FEEL SORRY FOR YOU - FAKE ILLNESS SO THEY FEEL REALLY WORRIED ABOUT YOU.

3. MAKE THEM WISH YOU HADN'T BEEN BORN - BECOME SO IRRITATING AND UPSET THEY WILL BE

TREADING ON EGGSHELLS, BECAUSE THEY WON'T WANT TO UPSET YOU - AND THEY'LL REALIZE THE IMPORTANCE OF BEING NICE TO UGENIA LAVENDER THE ONE AND ONLY CHILD.

4. MAKE THEM MISS YOU - SULK, IGNORE THEM COMPLETELY, TAKE A VOW OF SILENCE.

'That's a great plan of action!' said Ugenia as she smiled hopefully at the vision board. Their mission-impossible meeting was now over, and Rudy began to clear up the leftover sweet wrappers and empty glasses of tarberry juice.

☆

That very evening, Ugenia decided to put the mission impossible into action. Instead of vegging out in front of the television with Misfit, she began to prepare dinner, which involved helping Granny Betty chop vegetables, grate cheese, wash the fruit, unload the dishwasher, stir the soup, lay the table and dust the furniture.

After dinner, Ugenia stacked the dishwasher, cleaned the kitchen floor and even put a new black bin-liner in the rubbish bin.

The next morning, which was Saturday, instead of going out with Crazy Trevor to play football (which Ugenia loved to do), she made everyone breakfast – scrambled eggs on toast – then she vacuumed the dining room, lounge and stair carpet, polished the china ornaments, wiped the mirrors, washed the windows inside and out, made everyone's beds and cleaned the bathroom.

That afternoon, instead of going to Bronte's house to paint her toenails silver and eat homemade chocolate brownies (which Ugenia really wanted to do), she gritted her teeth and put on a pair of gloves, weeded the garden, collected the dead fallen leaves and swept up the front garden. Then she put the rubbish out and all the Christmas decorations up.

That evening, Rudy rang to see if Ugenia wanted to a watch a rerun of a Hunk Roberts movie – *The Return of the Killer Onion Savages, part two* (Ugenia's ultimate favourite) – but Ugenia was too tired even to do that.

'Rudy, making them need me is exhausting and they haven't even noticed,' she said furiously as she rubbed her eyes. 'My dad is too busy rubbing my mother's feet and my mother is too busy rubbing her belly.' And with that, Ugenia fell, exhausted, into bed.

☆

The next day Ugenia rolled out of bed, and as she brushed her teeth she gave herself a miserable toothpaste-advert smile. It's time for mission impossible number two, thought Ugenia – making them feel sorry for me. Ugenia stared in the mirror and tried to practise her best 'poor me' sick face.

Ugenia then climbed into bed and

pretended to feel ill as she rubbed her brow and gave a moan. She lay in bed for what felt like hours but was actually only three and a half minutes, feeling very restless.

Ugenia decided to moan out loud, but still nobody came. She grabbed some talc and rubbed it on her face. Then she walked into the bathroom, sprinkled her brow with water and went downstairs to where her mother and father were watching TV and eating toast in the lounge.

'I'm not well,' announced Ugenia.

'You do look a bit pale,' said her mother.

Ugenia sighed then wiped her damp forehead.

'You're sweating!' said Professor Lavender. 'Do you have a fever?'

'Maybe,' groaned Ugenia as she held her stomach and yelped. 'Ooh, I have a stomach ache.' Ugenia then made her ankles go floppy, and slightly crumpled her calves, then her thighs, then her waist, until she flopped completely on to the couch with her best pretend faint ever. (Ugenia resisted the temptation to open one eye to check her parents were watching.)

'You poor thing, Ugenia,' said her mother. 'Go back to bed immediately.'

'Don't worry about Ugenia,' said Granny Betty, coming into the room. 'I'll take care of her. Pandora . . . Edward, you get ready for your antenatal birth-breathing class.'

'That's such a shame,' said Pandora Lavender. 'We were planning to go to the hot-chocolate chunky-wonky doughnut stand before it, but Granny's right, Ugenia, you need to stay in bed and rest.'

'Injustice!' groaned Ugenia as she stomped upstairs and went to bed. 'This really isn't going to plan,' she sighed as she climbed under her Hunk Roberts duvet cover.

There was a little knock and Granny Betty poked her head around the door. 'Ugenia, I have some medicine to make you feel better.'

Granny Betty then entered the room,

poured out a large spoonful of brown medicine and tried to put it in Ugenia's mouth. It smelt of cheesy socks and vomit.

'Er, I'm feeling much better already, thanks, I really don't need any,' said Ugenia as she quickly ducked under the duvet.

'Ah, that's my girl!' said Granny Betty before going back downstairs.

This isn't going as I expected, thought Ugenia. I need to put mission-impossible three into action . . . make them wish I'd never been born!

Ugenia used her recovery time to think of ways she could be so obnoxiously bad that her parents would realize the importance of Ugenia. She could always behave a bit nicer if they treated her a little bit more special in future.

So that afternoon, when her parents came home from their antenatal class, Ugenia announced her speedy recovery and then began to implement some horrendous behaviour which was:

1. Emptying the shampoo bottle and replacing it with salad cream.
2. Putting laxatives in her dad's tea.
3. Hiding her mother's stretch-mark cream.
4. Leaving the bath running.
5. Turning up the music really loud every time her parents used the phone.

But to Ugenia's horror, none of this seemed to have the desired effect. Her parents didn't get angry with her so Ugenia could remind them to be nicer to her in future. They just seemed to carry on as if nothing had happened.

Ugenia had run out of ideas of alternative disruptive behaviour, but her parents seemed to be quite oblivious to anything other than getting ready for the new baby anyway. In fact, all it did was make Ugenia feel even more unimportant than before.

Ugenia went to bed very tired that evening – being horrendous was quite exhausting.

The next day, Ugenia leaped out of bed with a slight bounce in her step – it was her last few days of school and she was quite excited. Even though she still had Lara Slater to deal with, it was better than being around the boring, selfish baby growing inside her mother.

It was the day of the Christmas carol concert and nativity play. Miss Medina, the drama teacher, reminded them all that it started at three thirty and would be over by five o'clock.

Ugenia was a shepherdess along with Lara Slater – both of them had gone for the leading-lady role, but Miss Medina had decided that they both needed to take a back seat for this production and give someone else a chance. Miss Medina had chosen the new girl, Louisa Pegg, to play Mary. Will Darcy, as usual, was the leading man, Joseph. Rudy was the fairy angel on the Christmas tree, and Crazy Trevor was playing the newborn baby Jesus in the manger.

Ugenia was not entirely happy with any of the production . . .

1. She didn't want to be a shepherdess with a tea towel wrapped around her head. It was very unglamorous.
2. She didn't want to have to stand next to Lara Slater for an hour and a half.
3. She didn't want to be reminded about another selfish baby being born and stealing all the attention from everyone else.

After lessons were over, the school assembly

hall filled up with everyone's parents. Ugenia's class buzzed around getting ready for the concert.

At three thirty, when everyone was seated, Ugenia took her place next to Lara in the choir, ready to sing the first Christmas carol. Ugenia stared out into the crowd, looking for her parents, but she couldn't see them. Her mother and father had said they may come, depending on how Pandora was feeling.

'Silent Niiiiiight,' sang Lara at the top of her voice. 'Lonely infant with NO

MOTHER and child,' grinned Lara knowingly. 'Ooh dear . . . haven't they showed up for you,' she whispered.

'All is calm . . . all is BRIGHT,' sang Ugenia, trying her best to put on a brave face, as if it didn't matter.

After all the carols, Ugenia did her best shepherdess walk along with Lara, visiting the pretend baby Trevor in the manger covered with straw.

Ugenia stared at Trevor lying in the crib and began to wonder where exactly the selfish new baby would be sleeping when it finally came.

At the end of the service, Ugenia waited outside the school gates. It was very dark. She waited and she waited for what felt like hours (it was actually thirty minutes), until nearly everyone had gone. Miss Medina came out and waited with her. 'Your father's just rung to say he's been held up. Don't worry, I'm sure he'll be here soon,' she said.

Ugenia sighed with embarrassment when suddenly she saw her father's car pull up.

'I'm so sorry I'm late, Ugenia,' Professor Lavender puffed. 'I got held up . . . I was trying to get the baby's room ready before it arrives—'

'What room would that be then?' asked Ugenia.

'Didn't your mother tell you?' said Ugenia's father. 'We're converting your den into the baby's nursery. She said she was going to explain.'

Ugenia felt so angry and hurt she thought she was going to explode.

'Injustice! I'm the one and only child in this family! That's my room! I hate you!' she screamed at the top of her voice.

Mr Lavender looked tired and tense. He took a deep breath and tried calmly to steer Ugenia into the car. 'Ugenia, we realize this new baby coming has been very hard on you, but we don't want to stress your mother out, do we? Look, how about we drive up to Garrods Department Store on Christmas Eve to meet Father Christmas to make up for it?'

'Dad, I don't care about meeting Father Christmas, I'm too old!' snapped Ugenia as she sat in the back and Mr Lavender started to drive off.

'Come on, don't be like that. I'm not too old to meet Father Christmas,' said

Professor Lavender, trying to be funny. 'And I'm forty!'

Ugenia gave her father a weak smile and they drove home in silence. Ugenia thought quietly to herself. Right, it's time for mission-impossible four. Make them miss me.

That night, Ugenia gave the best sulk you could ever imagine. She gave the blackest, darkest look and the deepest sigh, as if to say no one understands a single thing I'm going through. Unfortunately this did not produce the desired effect that Ugenia wanted. Her parents still didn't seem to notice.

☆

So here they were, a few days later, driving down Boxmore Hill, past the twenty-four-hour, bargain-budget, bulk-buyers' supersized supermarket. It was Christmas Eve and, as promised, Professor Lavender was taking Ugenia to see Father Christmas. Pandora Lavender had gone with them, with her big swollen belly. As they drew up outside the store, Professor Lavender nodded politely to the doorman, who was wearing a matching purple coat and top hat. Garrods wasn't just any old shop. Garrods was spectacular. It sold everything from shoes to sofas, celery to satchels, books to baggage, pants to potatoes. It even sold scented purple toilet paper to wipe pet pooches' bottoms.

That day it was particularly busy as all the late Christmas shoppers were there, buying their last-minute pressies and queuing up to meet Father Christmas.

Ugenia, Pandora and Edward went up to the toy floor to join the Father Christmas queue. Reluctantly Ugenia held Professor Lavender's camera, ready to give to the elf to take her picture with Father Christmas.

But as they reached the end of the queue, a small man in a green elf suit hung out a sign that said: TEA BREAK – FATHER

CHRISTMAS WILL BE BACK LATER.

'Oh dear,' said Pandora. 'What a shame. Still, we can come back in a bit. Let's do a bit of shopping to pass the time. The baby section is just over there.'

'What? Shopping but not for ME? Injustice!' huffed Ugenia. 'I need the loo,' she said, feeling like it was probably best to step out of the situation before she really threw a strop and stressed her mother out. Besides, none of her tactics seemed to be working and, if anything, her mission impossible had only seemed to make her feel worse. Ugenia stood among the crowded shoppers and watched her mother with the greedy selfish baby in her belly waddle off in a trance towards the baby department.

'Oooh, they have such cute little baby clothes!' Pandora Lavender was calling over her shoulder.

Ugenia shrugged her shoulders. I might as well not be here, she thought. Things suddenly did feel worse – Ugenia not only felt unimportant, she felt invisible.

'Dad, I'll be back in a minute,' said Ugenia as she left him with his wife, staring at pink and blue baby bonnets.

Ugenia wandered into a cubicle in the ladies' toilet. Ugenia was just about to take a pee, when she suddenly realized there was no toilet paper.

'Not again!' said Ugenia.

She stepped outside the cubicle, where a lady in a white overall was handing out paper towels over by the mirror.

'You've run out of loo paper!' said Ugenia crossly.

'Ooh, I'm sorry,' said the lady, handing her a big new loo roll. 'It's one of those things – it's not until something's missing that you really appreciate how important it is . . .'

Ugenia stared at the loo roll. Suddenly, like a thunderbolt of lightning, she had a brainwave. Inspirational! I need to *really* go missing, maybe then they'll appreciate me properly, thought Ugenia.

Ugenia didn't need the loo any more. In fact, she was too busy charging out of the toilets, down the golden escalator, out of Garrods and into the street. Ugenia wandered up the back alley behind the department store and sat on a wall. Ha, that'll teach 'em. They'll be sorry now I've gone forever, thought Ugenia as she crossed her arms proudly.

One minute later, Ugenia felt a little bit cold as she began to think of all the things she would miss. There was her dog, Misfit, and her friends too. No more Hunk Roberts movies or Granny Betty . . . she'd even miss her parents.

Suddenly, Ugenia didn't feel so angry any more – in fact she felt a bit sad.

The temperature was dropping, snowflakes began to fall on her cheeks, frost began to bite her nose and her teeth began to chatter. Ugenia was feeling really glum and lonely, when suddenly, out of the corner of her eye, she spotted a large man with a white beard, wearing a red suit.

It was Father Christmas, sitting on the wall and sipping a cup of tea from a paper cup.

'Hey, what's up, kid,' said Father Christmas with a husky American accent.

Ugenia paused. This Father Christmas sounded very familiar . . .

'Nothing, I'm just a bit fed up, that's all,' said Ugenia. 'Anyway, what's it to do with you?' she asked defensively. 'And why aren't you upstairs working? Father

Christmas shouldn't be taking time out!'

'Every Father Christmas needs a bit of a break,' said this Father Christmas. 'I feel a little stressed out.'

'Stressed out? It's me that's stressed out! I'm not taking a break and my life is currently ruined!' Suddenly Ugenia began to tell this Father Christmas everything, and once she started, she couldn't stop – all the injustices: the Hollywood trip and not meeting Hunk Roberts; her den being transformed into a nursery; her parents not coming to the play and forgetting to pick her up; feeling ignored and invisible . . . 'And now I have to go missing so my parents will remember how important I am and it's all because of that stupid, selfish baby!'

'I hope you don't mind me saying this,' said the Father Christmas, 'but it sounds like it's YOU that's being the selfish baby!' He pulled off his beard, revealing a slightly chiselled chin and familiar handsome brown eyes.

Ugenia gulped as she heard these words from a very, very familiar face. It was her favourite action hero, HUNK ROBERTS!

'You . . . you might be right,' gulped Ugenia, who suddenly felt like a bit of a big selfish baby. Then she stopped herself. 'Hey, but hang on a minute. What on earth are you, Hunk Roberts, doing being Father Christmas?'

'Well, things have been going a bit slow with my movie career recently,' said Hunk. 'There's a new kid on the block – Bradley Litt. It hasn't been going so well, so I decided to take this job. I have to accept change like everyone else. But actually it's made me realize that I've got to make room for someone younger to come along and also how lucky I've been in the past. Sometimes in life you have to step out of what you're doing to realize how great things are.'

'Do you know what,' said Ugenia, who suddenly realized that she was getting rather cold and that her parents might have missed her (although Ugenia had been gone for only nineteen and a half minutes). 'I think you might be right. Thanks, Hunk, I think I'd better be going back to my life inside! Ooh, and one more thing,' said Ugenia. 'It's great to finally meet the real Hunk Roberts! May I have a picture?'

Hunk got up off the wall and smiled with Ugenia as they got a passer-by to take their photo.

Ugenia then ran back through the large doors into the building. Garrods was now extra busy, so Ugenia charged up the golden escalator and back to the baby department. But her parents were nowhere to be seen. Suddenly, Ugenia bumped into a tiny moon-faced man in a purple tailored suit. It was Alfred, the owner of the department store, who she had met a while ago when she was shopping with Bronte and her mother, Pamela.

'Ugenia, thank goodness I've found you,' shrieked Alfred hysterically. 'Follow me.'

Ugenia quickly followed Alfred through the sportswear section and into the bedroom department to see her mother lying peacefully on one of the large display beds, surrounded by her father, a few passing shoppers and Doctor Clooney (who she had met before, when her parents had a car accident).

'Ugenia, thank goodness,' cried Pandora. 'It's so important that you're here for this special moment! It all happened so quickly.'

Ugenia stared at her mother sitting up among the white fluffy pillows, holding a small bundle in her arms.

'It was a miracle that Doctor Clooney just happened to be shopping, so he could help,' said Professor Lavender.

'Congratulations, Ugenia,' said Doctor Clooney. 'Meet your new baby brother.'

Ugenia smiled at the little baby boy, who looked like a rather cute wrinkled raisin wrapped in some peach-coloured bath towels from the bathroom department.

'Ugenia, I hope you won't be bothered about no longer being the one and only child,' chuckled Doctor Clooney.

'Me? Bothered?' beamed Ugenia. 'Nah, I'm not bothered about being the one and only child. Besides, I'm still the one and only GIRL!'

uGenia Lavender

Big News!

BIG NEWS . . . BIG NEWS . . .
BIGGEST NEWS EVER!

CAN YOU BELIEVE I HAVE A LITTLE BROTHER? I AM THE BIG SISTER!

So things didn't turn out so bad after all – we ended up having

Christmas lunch with Doctor Clooney and Alfred, the owner of Garrods, who invited HUNK ROBERTS!

So I did finally meet him properly in the end! And having a new baby brother around is actually quite cool, although I'm not sure about the stinky nappies . . . phew . . .

So it's been a fabulous year – loads of amazing things have happened. And you've been on my adventures with me – the art-gallery robbery, the Lovely Illness, the film set, meeting the alien . . . so much. I think the best bit about it was being able to share it with you. I hope you enjoyed it – let me know which was your favourite. Fingers crossed, we can do it again. Except next time it'll be an even BIGGER adventure!

Thanks for being there. See ya.

Big XO
Love, your friend forever . . .
Ugenia Estelle Lavender xx
PS I only tell my best friend my middle name.

uGenia Lavender

Ingenious Top Tip

Everything happens for a reason . . .

Look how angry I was about not going to Hollywood, but thank goodness I didn't go – I definitely wouldn't have got to meet Hunk Roberts, as he was here! See, everything always turns out for the best in the end! Sad to say goodbye!

Brain Squeezers

Ugenia's Energy-Saving Tips

You know, we can all do our little bit to help save the planet. For starters, my teacher, Mr Columbus, told us lots of *ingenious* ways to save energy around the home. Can you choose the right word to complete each of these helpful tips?

1. Take a ______ instead of a bath. It uses less water!

2. Recycle all your _______.

3. Turn ___ the lights when you leave a room.

4. If you can, ____ to school instead of going by car.

5. Don't leave the ___ running when you brush your teeth.

6. Switch off the __ when you've finished watching it.

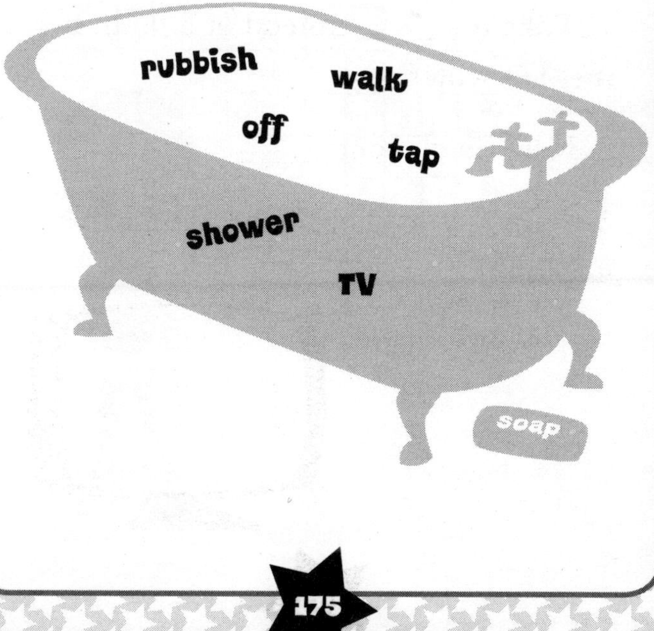

Ugenia's Super Space Crossword

Wow! Meeting a strange creature from another planet certainly opened my eyes to the wonders of the universe! How much do you know about what's 'out there'? Try my super space crossword to find out.

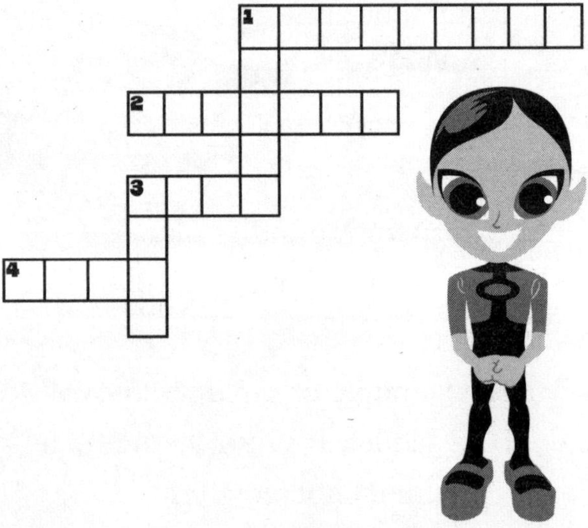

ACROSS

1. A person who travels into space has to wear a special suit and is called an __________.

2. When the moon passes through the earth's shadow, the sky goes completely dark. This exciting event is called a lunar ________.

3. It can be round or crescent-shaped, and it comes out at night.

4. 'Twinkle, twinkle, little ____.'

DOWN

1. A creature from another planet. I think Edie Titchmarsh might have been one of these!

3. This is the name of a planet known as the Red Planet. It's also the name of a rather yummy chocolate bar!

Ugenia's Pet Shop Wordsnake

Aaww! Rudy really loved his pet gerbil, Germaine. Do you love pets too? If so, try to find nine pets hidden in this winding wordsnake. The words go in one continuous line, snaking up and down, backwards and forwards, but never diagonally, in the same order as the list below.

BUDGIE

GERBIL

FISH

CAT

DOG

MOUSE

HAMSTER

SNAKE

RABBIT

Tip! Use a pencil in case you make a mistake. Then you can just start again!

Start here

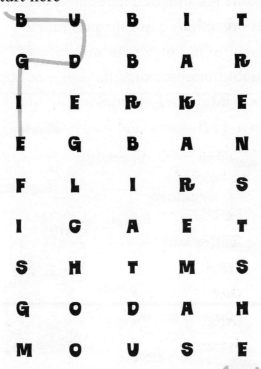

B	U	B	I	T
G	D	B	A	R
I	E	R	K	E
E	G	B	A	N
F	L	I	R	S
I	C	A	E	T
S	H	T	M	S
G	O	D	A	H
M	O	U	S	E

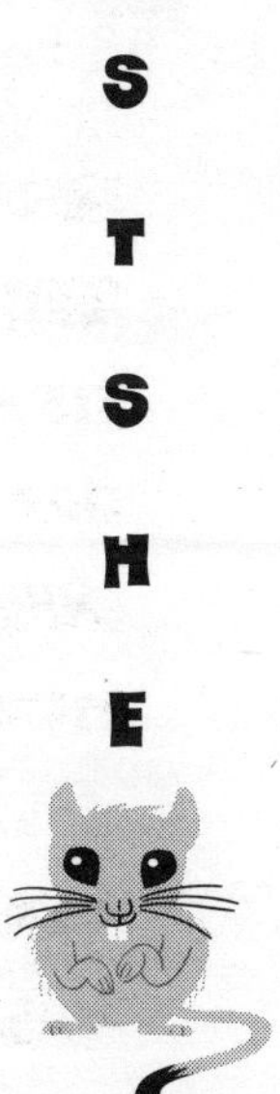

Ugenia's Baby Mix-Up

I've just been shopping with my mum at Garrods, but we've dropped our bags and everything's got mixed up! She's bought things for the new baby and I've bought things for myself. Can you help by circling all *my* things?

blanket

nappies

bracelet

lipgloss

trainers

bottle of milk

changing mat

dummy

pram

mobile phone

rucksack

computer game

giant chocolate bar

rattle

Answers

Ugenia's Energy-Saving Tips

1. shower
2. rubbish
3. off
4. walk
5. tap
6. TV

Ugenia's Super Space Crossword

ACROSS

1. ASTRONAUT
2. ECLIPSE
3. MOON
4. STAR

DOWN

1. ALIEN
3. MARS

Ugenia's Pet Shop Wordsnake

B	U	B	I	T
G	D	B	A	R
I	E	R	K	E
E	G	B	A	N
F	L	I	R	S
I	C	A	E	T
S	H	T	M	S
G	O	D	A	H
M	O	U	S	E

Ugenia's Baby Mix-Up

Ugenia's things: bracelet, trainers, lipgloss, mobile phone, rucksack, computer game, giant chocolate bar.

uGenia Lavender

Ugenia Lavender starts a new school, meets swoony Will Darcy and rescues a celebrity chef from a big messy mix-up!

Ugenia Lavender visits the circus, goes on Breakfast TV and has to turn a TERRIBLE TIGER into a pussycat!

uGenia Lavender

Ugenia Lavender has a birthday surprise, runs in the Olympics and saves the world from some BURNING PANTS!

Ugenia Lavender stars in a movie, rides the Death Wish at Lunar Park and plans a feast for her friends when she's HOME ALONE!

uGenia Lavender

Ugenia Lavender meets a giant, rescues her parents from a blood-sucking vampire and has to escape from the TEMPLE OF GLOOM!

Ugenia Lavender saves the planet, helps an alien and stops being THE ONE AND ONLY!